Bears and a Birthday

Shirley Parenteau

illustrated by David Walker

WALKER BOOKS
AND SUBSIDIARIES
LONDON · BOSTON · SYDNEY · AUCKLAND

The makings for
a cake are there.
The recipe's ready.
Where are the bears?

Fuzzy and Floppy
come running in.
"Let's go!" they call.
"Let's all begin!"

Yellow and Calico
find a spoon.
"Hurry! Hurry!
He'll be here soon!"

Four small bears
measure and pour.

Who can they
be baking for?

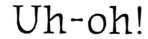

Uh-oh!

A knock at the door!
It's Big Brown Bear!
He calls, "What smells
so good in there?"

Floppy looks out with
flour on her chin.
"Sorry, Big Bear.
Too soon to come in!"

They fill the pans.
It's time to bake.

This will be
a perfect cake!

Now for a gift!
They wrap a ball.
Be careful there.
Don't let it fall!

Oops!

Find more paper!
That piece tore.
Now the ball
is on the floor!

Big Bear smells
sugar and spice.
Are they baking
something nice?

He nudges the door
just a crack.
"No peeking!" they warn,
and nudge it back.

Big Brown Bear says,
"Pickle!" and "Pooh!"
But waiting is all
that bear can do!

At last!

The cake is ready.

The icing's spread.

They choose a candle,

tall and red.

The four bears shout,
"Surprise, Big Bear!
Here's why we
were busy in there!"

"It's all for you!"
calls Calico.
They offer the ball
with a bright-red bow.

What a smile
on Big Brown Bear!
He didn't know
how much they care!

Yay!
He blows out the candle
with a puff of air.
"Happy birthday,
Big Brown Bear!"

They play some games.
They laugh and sing
for Big Brown Bear,
the Birthday King!

For my sisters and brothers: Marjorie, Virgil, Paul
and Gail, for the birthdays we shared
S. P.

Especially for Masashi, with thanks for introducing
these bears to so many young book lovers
D. W.

First published 2016 by Walker Books Ltd
87 Vauxhall Walk, London SE11 5HJ

2 4 6 8 10 9 7 5 3 1

Text © 2016 Shirley Parenteau
Illustrations © 2016 David Walker

This book was typeset in Journal

Printed in China

British Library Cataloguing in Publication Data:
A catalogue record for this book is available from the British Library

ISBN 978-1-4063-7267-0

www.walker.co.uk